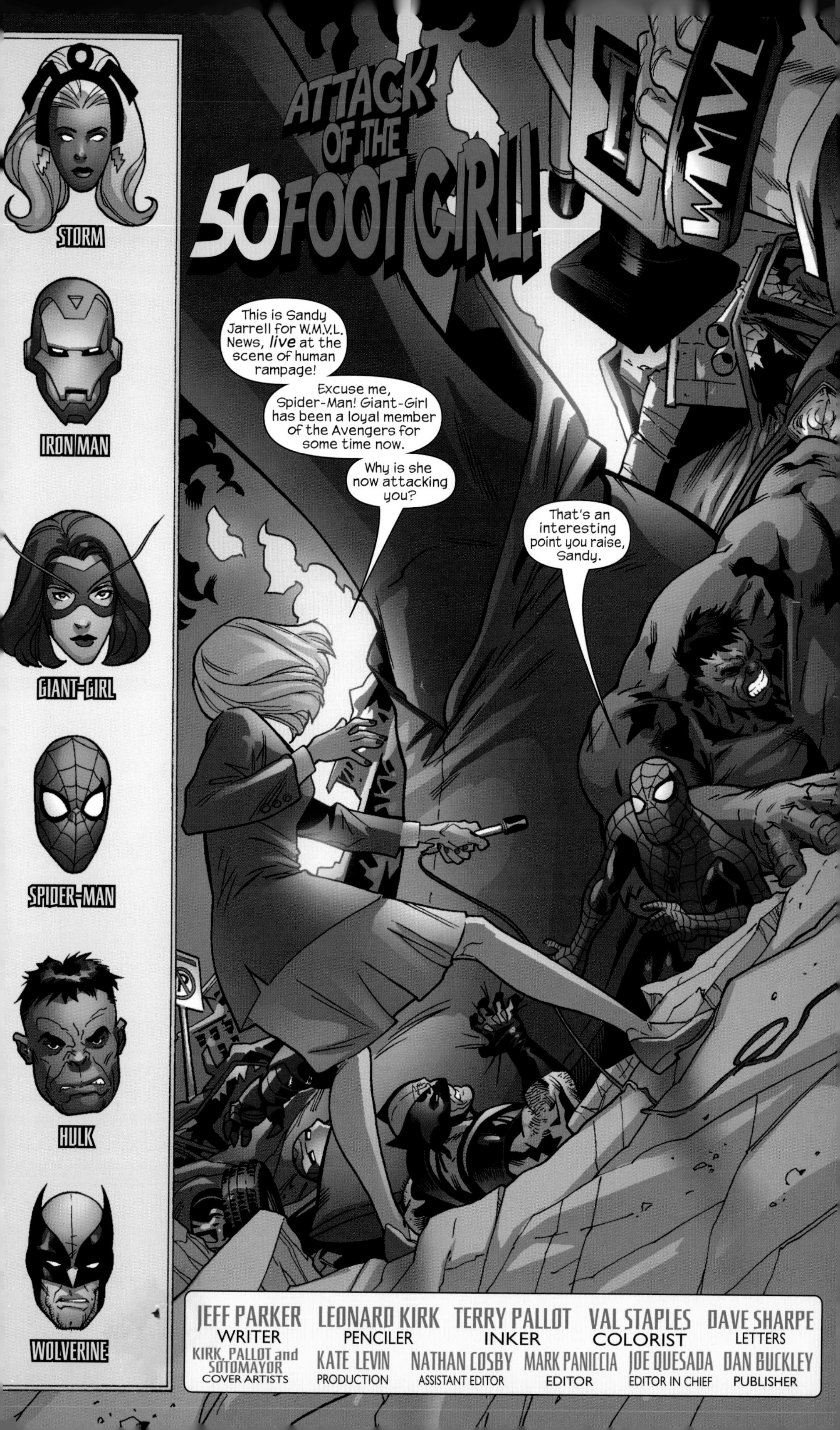

STORM
IRON MAN
GIANT-GIRL
SPIDER-MAN
HULK
WOLVERINE
ATTACK OF THE 50 FOOT GIRL!
This is Sandy Jarrell for W.M.V.L. News, live at the scene of human rampage!
Excuse me, Spider-Man! Giant-Girl has been a loyal member of the Avengers for some time now.
Why is she now attacking you?
That's an interesting point you raise, Sandy.
JEFF PARKER WRITER
LEONARD KIRK PENCILER
TERRY PALLOT INKER
VAL STAPLES COLORIST
DAVE SHARPE LETTERS
KIRK, PALLOT and SOTOMAYOR COVER ARTISTS
KATE LEVIN PRODUCTION
NATHAN COSBY ASSISTANT EDITOR
MARK PANICCIA EDITOR
JOE QUESADA EDITOR IN CHIEF
DAN BUCKLEY PUBLISHER

WWW.ABDOPUBLISHING.COM

Reinforced library bound edition published in 2015 by Spotlight, a division of ABDO, PO Box 398166, Minneapolis, Minnesota 55439. Spotlight produces high-quality reinforced library bound editions for schools and libraries. Published by agreement with Marvel Characters, Inc.

Printed in the United States of America, North Mankato, Minnesota.
052014
072014

THIS BOOK CONTAINS RECYCLED MATERIALS

MARVEL
Marvel.com

LIBRARY OF CONGRESS CATALOGING-IN-PUBLICATION DATA

Parker, Jeff, 1966-
The Avengers. set 4 / Jeff Parker, writer ; Leonard Park, penciler ; Terry Pallot, inker ; Val Staples, colorist ; Dave Sharpe, letters ; Kirk, Pallot, and Sotomayer, cover artists. -- Reinforced library bound edition.
pages cm
ISBN 978-1-61479-293-2 (Attack of the 50 foot girl!) -- ISBN 978-1-61479-294-9 (The avenging seven) -- ISBN 978-1-61479-295-6 (Bringers of the Storm) -- ISBN 978-1-61479-296-3 (Even a Hawkeye can cry!)
1. Graphic novels. I. Kirk, Leonard, illustrator. II. Pallot, Terry, illustrator. III. Sotomayor, Chris, illustrator. IV. Avengers (Comic strip) V. Title.
PZ7.7.P252Ave 2015
741.5'973--dc23

2014005384

ABDO
Spotlight

A Division of ABDO
www.abdopublishing.com

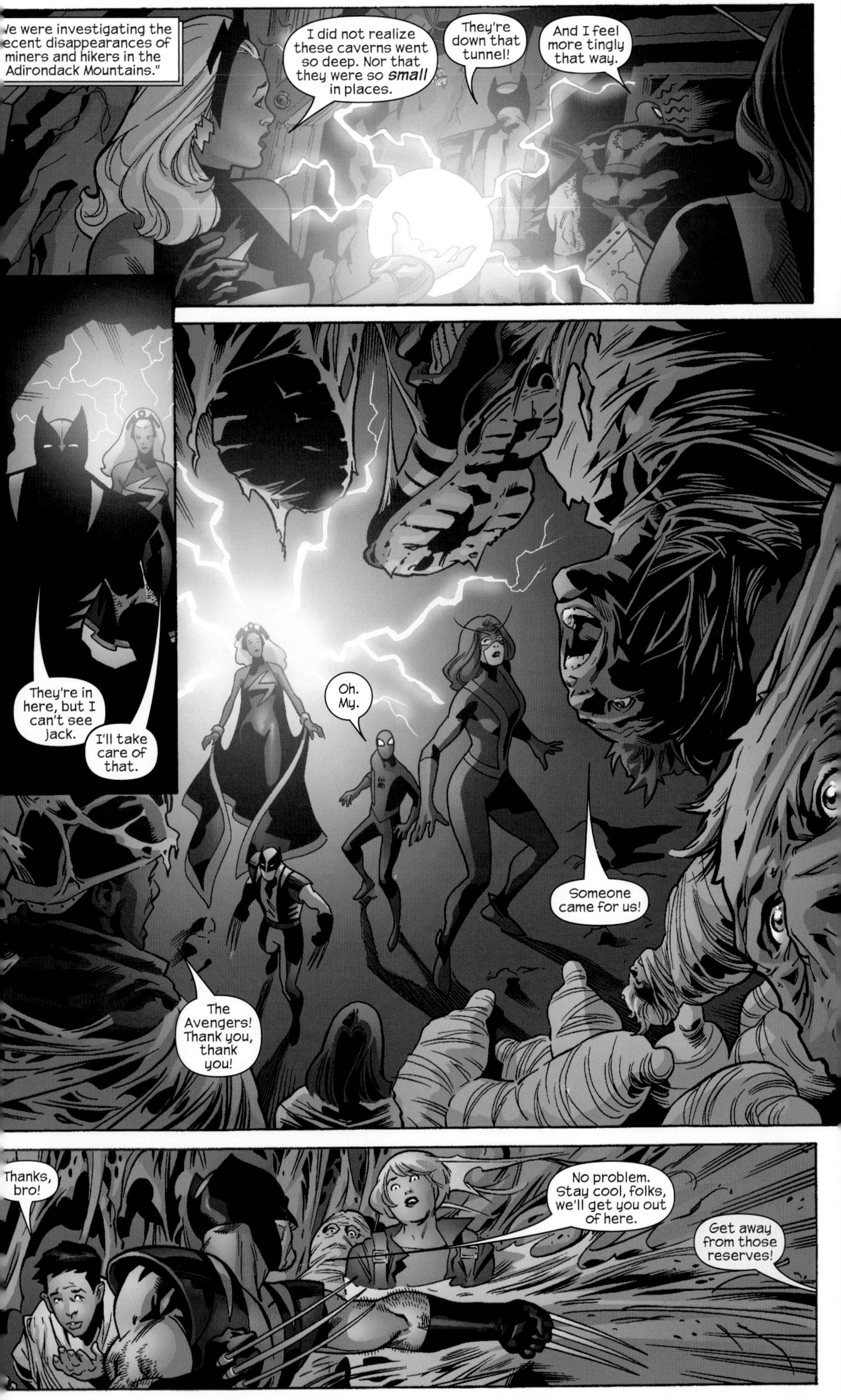

/e were investigating the ecent disappearances of miners and hikers in the Adirondack Mountains."
I did not realize these caverns went so deep. Nor that they were so *small* in places.
They're down that tunnel!
And I feel more tingly that way.
They're in here, but I can't see jack.
I'll take care of that.
Oh. My.
Someone came for us!
The Avengers! Thank you, thank you!
Thanks, bro!
No problem. Stay cool, folks, we'll get you out of here.
Get away from those reserves!

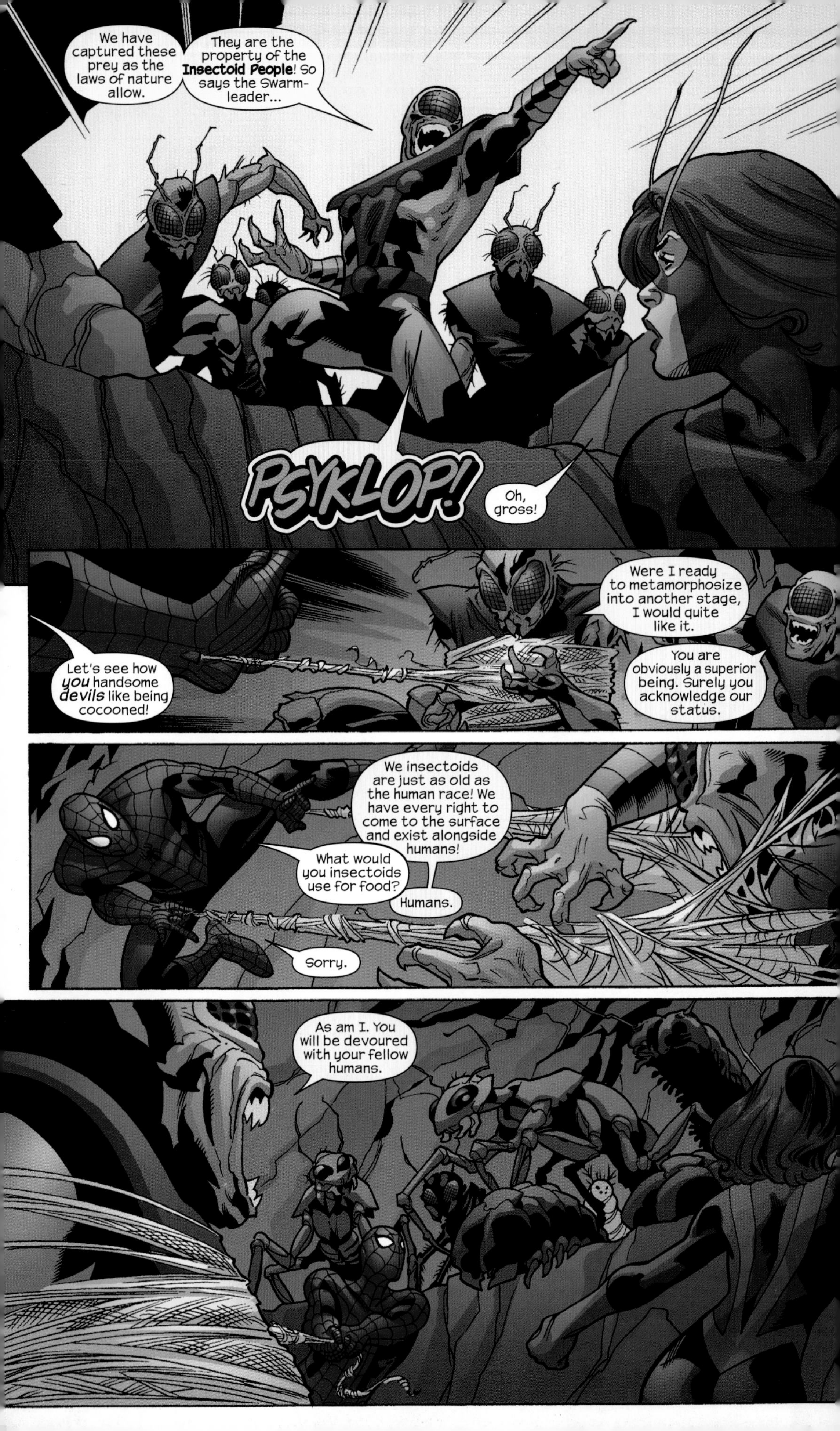

We have captured these prey as the laws of nature allow.
They are the property of the **Insectoid People**! So says the Swarm-leader...
PSYKLOP!
Oh, gross!
Let's see how *you* handsome *devils* like being cocooned!
Were I ready to metamorphosize into another stage, I would quite like it.
You are obviously a superior being. Surely you acknowledge our status.
We insectoids are just as old as the human race! We have every right to come to the surface and exist alongside humans!
What would you insectoids use for food?
Humans.
Sorry.
As am I. You will be devoured with your fellow humans.

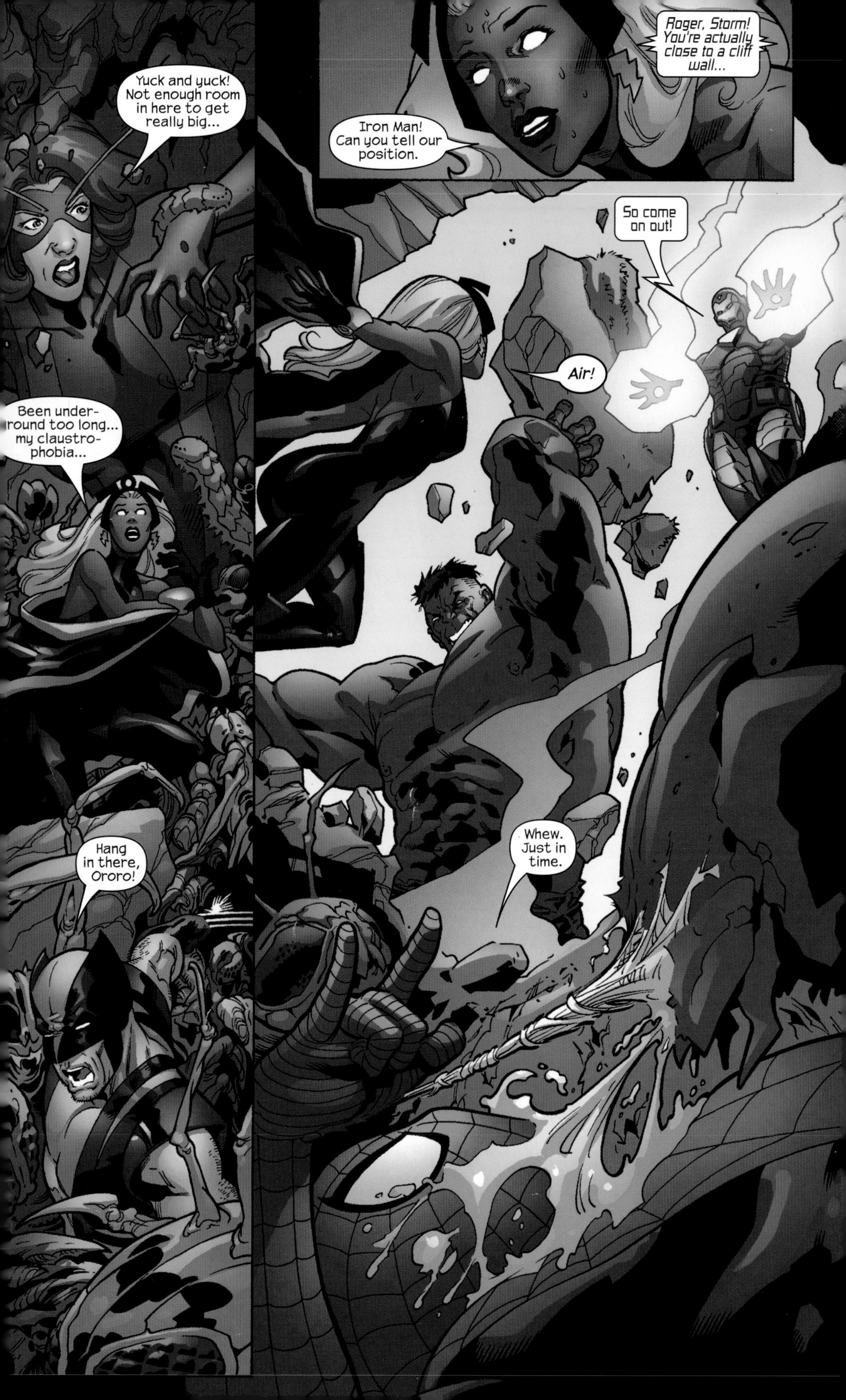
Yuck and yuck! Not enough room in here to get really big...
Been under-round too long... my claustro-phobia...
Hang in there, Ororo!
Iron Man! Can you tell our position.
Roger, Storm! You're actually close to a cliff wall...
So come on out!
Air!
Whew. Just in time.

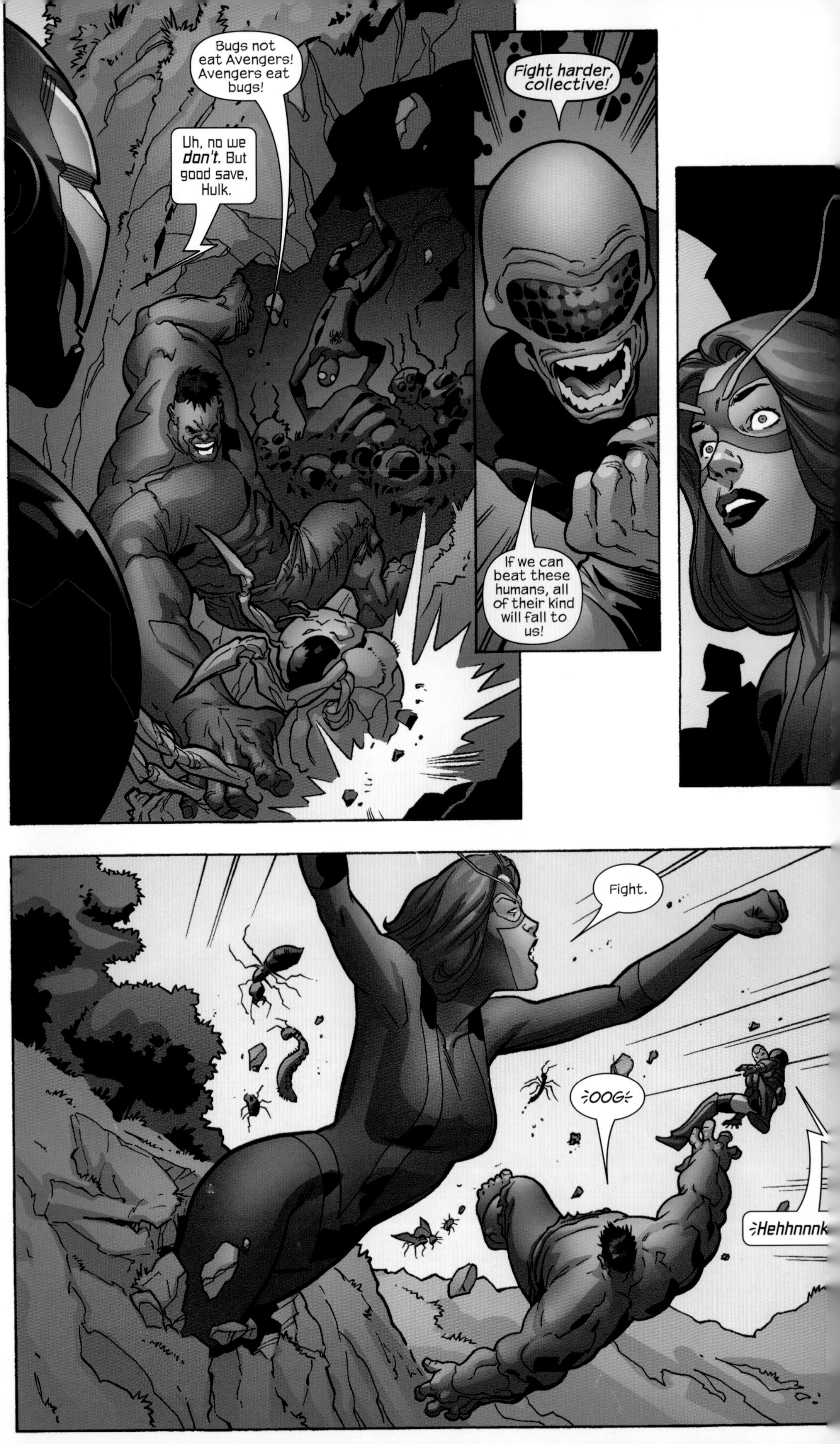
Bugs not eat Avengers! Avengers eat bugs!
Uh, no we *don't*. But good save, Hulk.
Fight harder, collective!
If we can beat these humans, all of their kind will fall to us!
Fight.
OOG
Hehhnnnk

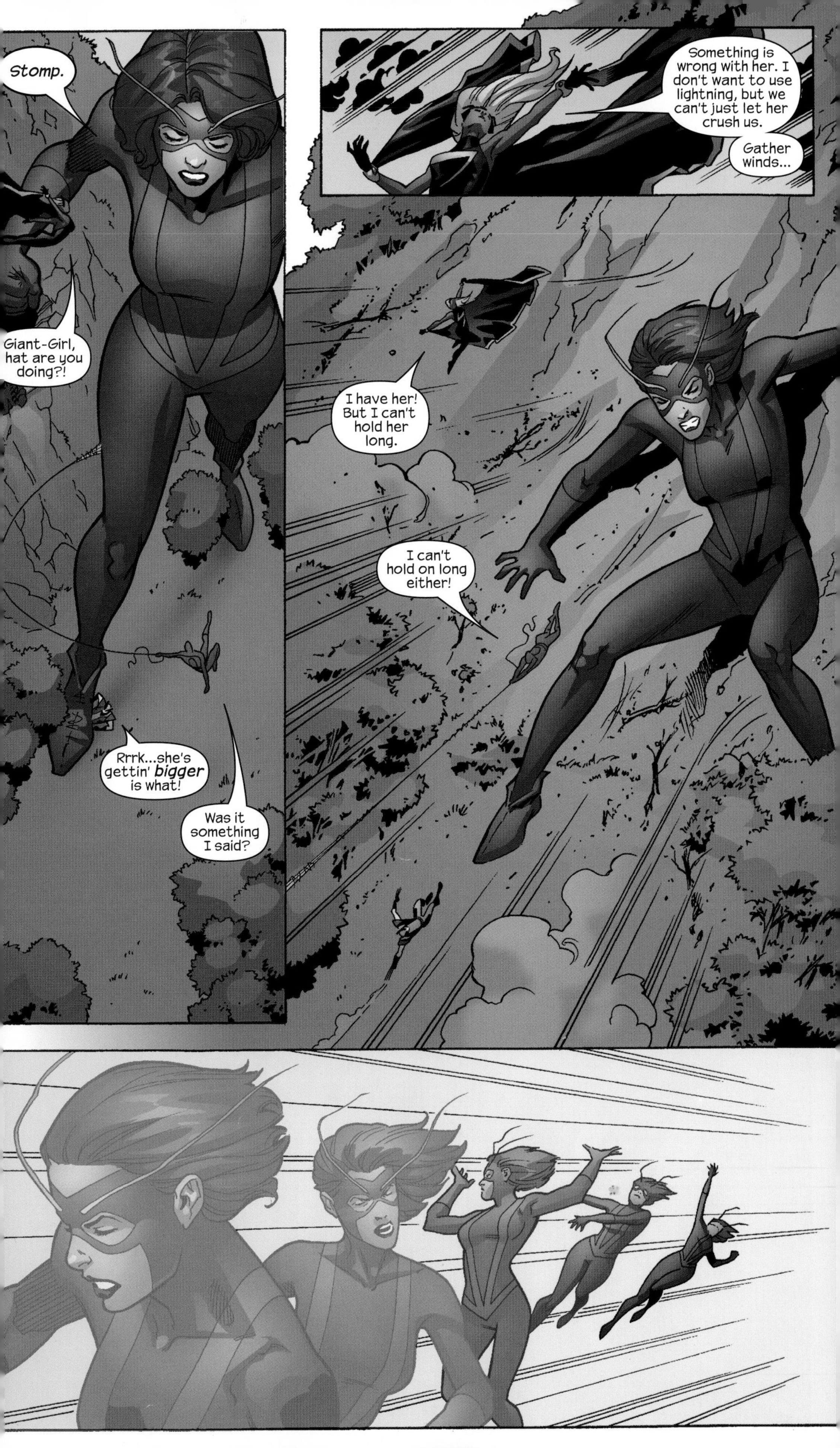
Stomp.
Giant-Girl, hat are you doing?!
Rrrk...she's gettin' *bigger* is what!
Was it something I said?
Something is wrong with her. I don't want to use lightning, but we can't just let her crush us.
Gather winds...
I have her! But I can't hold her long.
I can't hold on long either!

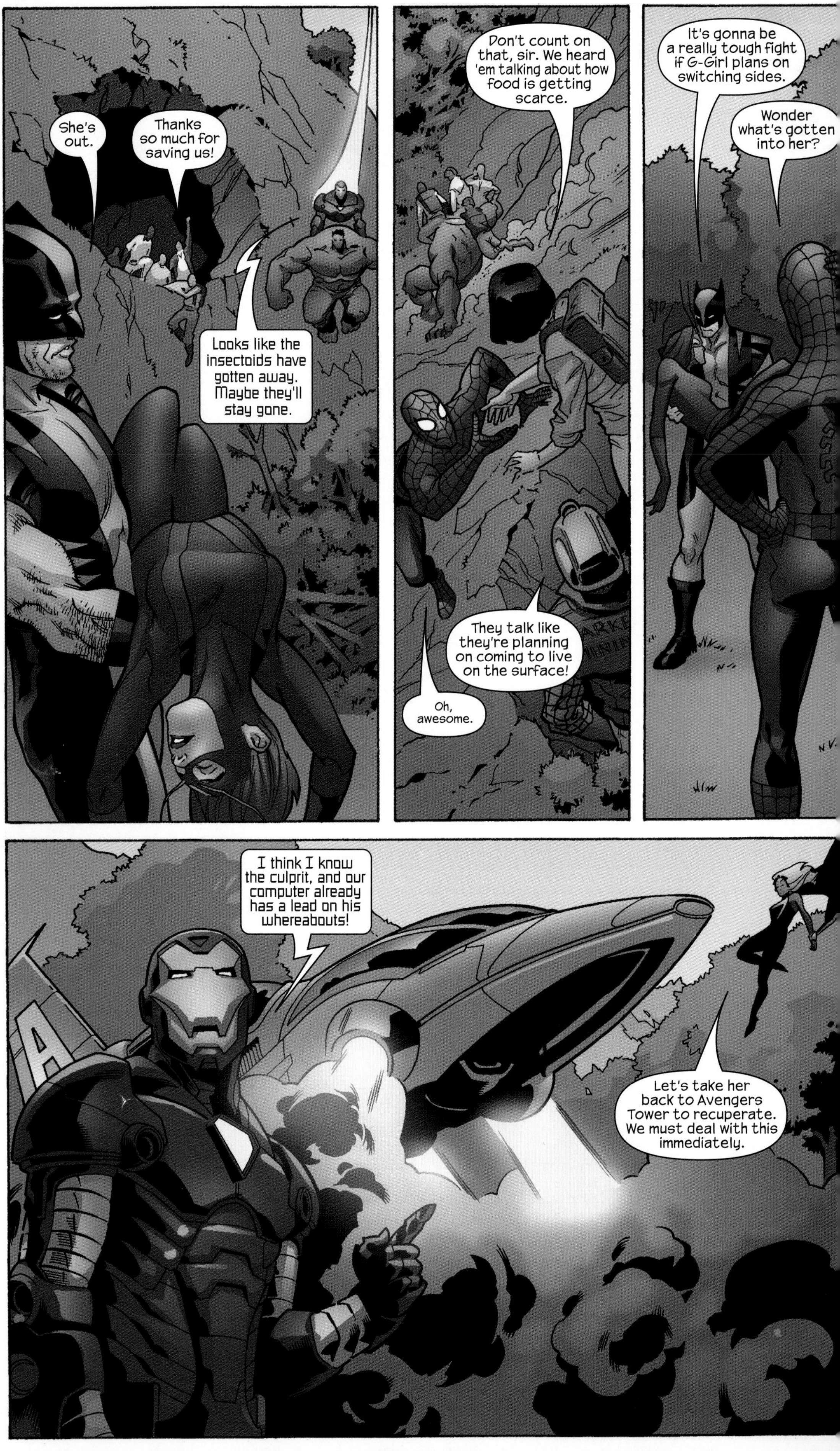
She's out.
Thanks so much for saving us!
Looks like the insectoids have gotten away. Maybe they'll stay gone.
Don't count on that, sir. We heard 'em talking about how food is getting scarce.
They talk like they're planning on coming to live on the surface!
Oh, awesome.
It's gonna be a really tough fight if G-Girl plans on switching sides.
Wonder what's gotten into her?
I think I know the culprit, and our computer already has a lead on his whereabouts!
Let's take her back to Avengers Tower to recuperate. We must deal with this immediately.

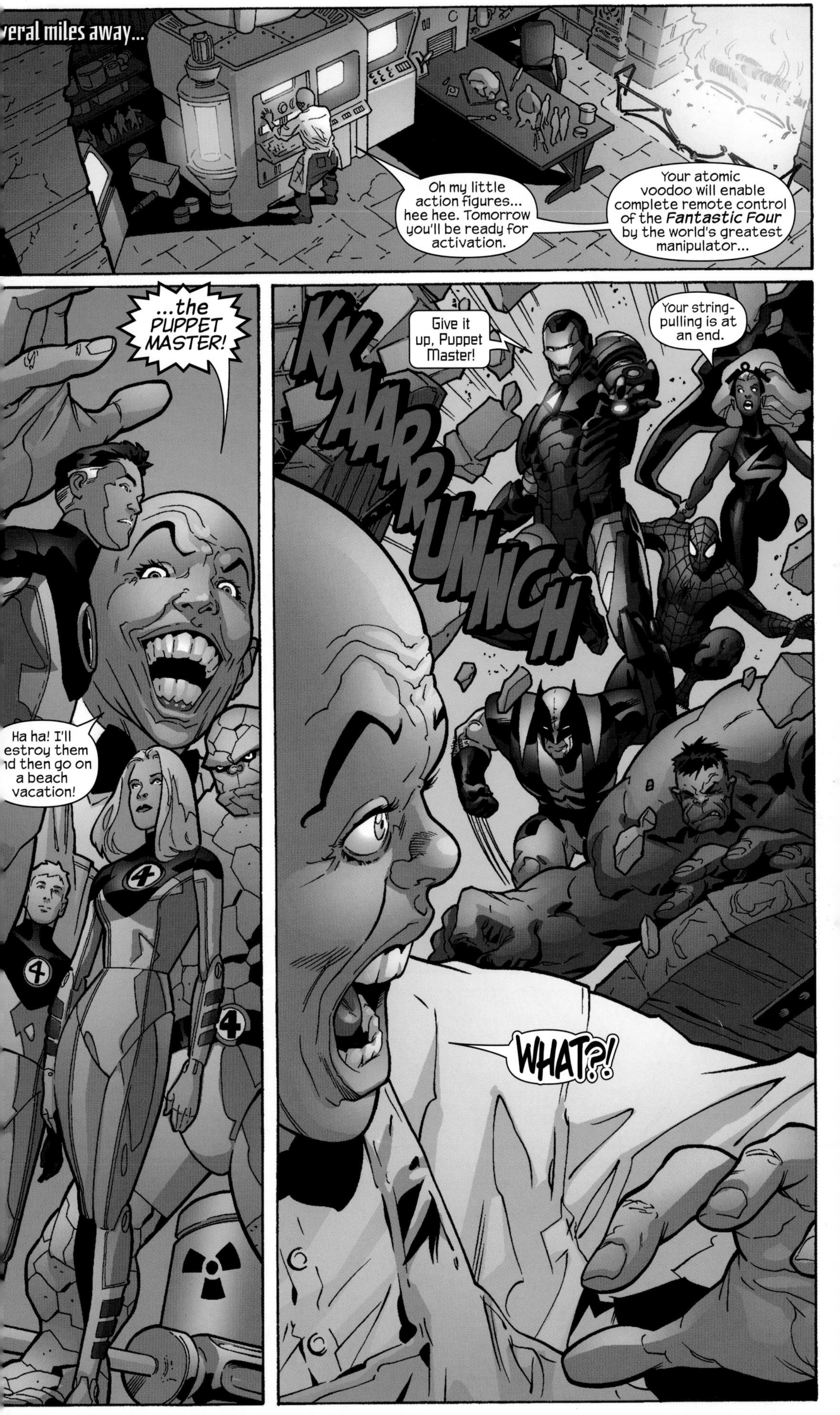
veral miles away...
Oh my little action figures... hee hee. Tomorrow you'll be ready for activation.
Your atomic voodoo will enable complete remote control of the *Fantastic Four* by the world's greatest manipulator...
...the PUPPET MASTER!
Ha ha! I'll estroy them nd then go on a beach vacation!
KKAARRUNNCH
Give it up, Puppet Master!
Your string-pulling is at an end.
WHAT?!

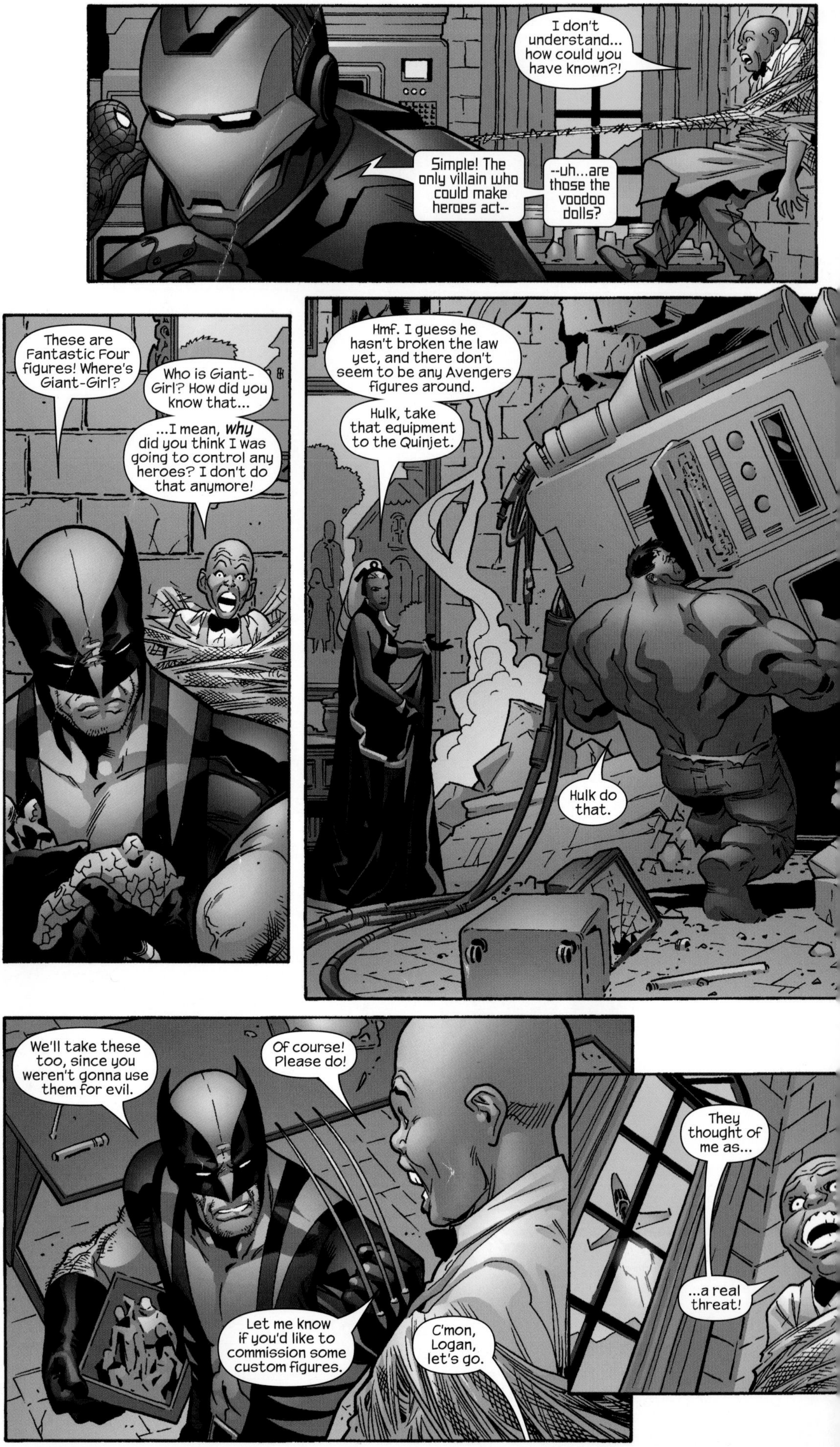
I don't understand... how could you have known?!
Simple! The only villain who could make heroes act--
--uh...are those the voodoo dolls?
These are Fantastic Four figures! Where's Giant-Girl?
Who is Giant-Girl? How did you know that...
...I mean, *why* did you think I was going to control any heroes? I don't do that anymore!
Hmf. I guess he hasn't broken the law yet, and there don't seem to be any Avengers figures around.
Hulk, take that equipment to the Quinjet.
Hulk do that.
We'll take these too, since you weren't gonna use them for evil.
Of course! Please do!
Let me know if you'd like to commission some custom figures.
C'mon, Logan, let's go.
They thought of me as...
...a real threat!

"As you might have figured, Giant-Girl didn't stay at headquarters."

Boy, is she on a tear!

We've *got* to get her outside of the city!

Don't worry, Storm, we'll contain her.

MANEUVER 4-A!

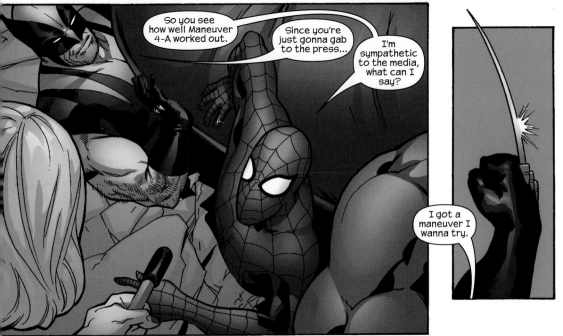

So you see how well Maneuver 4-A worked out.

Since you're just gonna gab to the press...

I'm sympathetic to the media, what can I say?

I got a maneuver I wanna try.

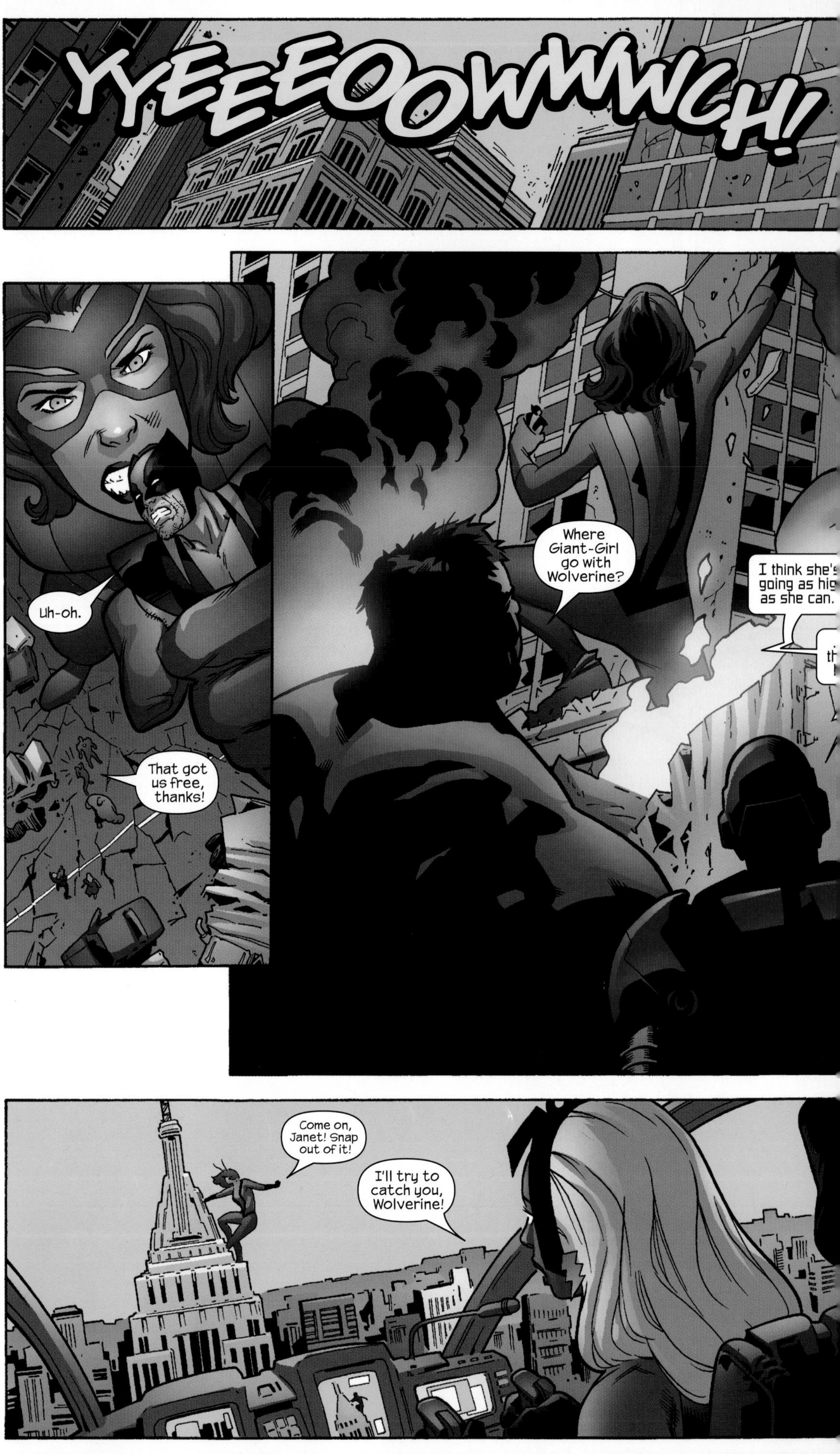
YYEEEOOWWWCH!
Uh-oh.
That got us free, thanks!
Where Giant-Girl go with Wolverine?
I think she' going as hig as she can.
Come on, Janet! Snap out of it!
I'll try to catch you, Wolverine!

RRRAARRH!

Think I'm about to get an air tour of New York...

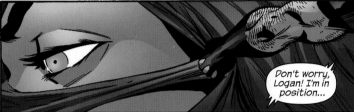

Don't worry, Logan! I'm in position...

...to catch you...

RRRIIIPPP

Copter 2! Go in close on her face!!

STOOOOOOOORRRRRMM

Breaking news! Climbing down the Empire State Building and at war with her team is Avenger Giant-Girl...

...now revealed to be wealthy socialite Janet Van Dyne!

This day just keeps getting worse.

KRONCH

Hey, where's she going?

There's no telling.

Hulk not blame Giant-Girl for this!

Hey, look what I found in the Hudson.

Shuddup.

Good. You two and Hulk will follow her. Try to keep her damage to a minimum.

Spider-Man and I will go talk to someone who knows her best.

I've put in a call to Ver Van Dyne.

Her fath

Ooool she's g to be trou-ble

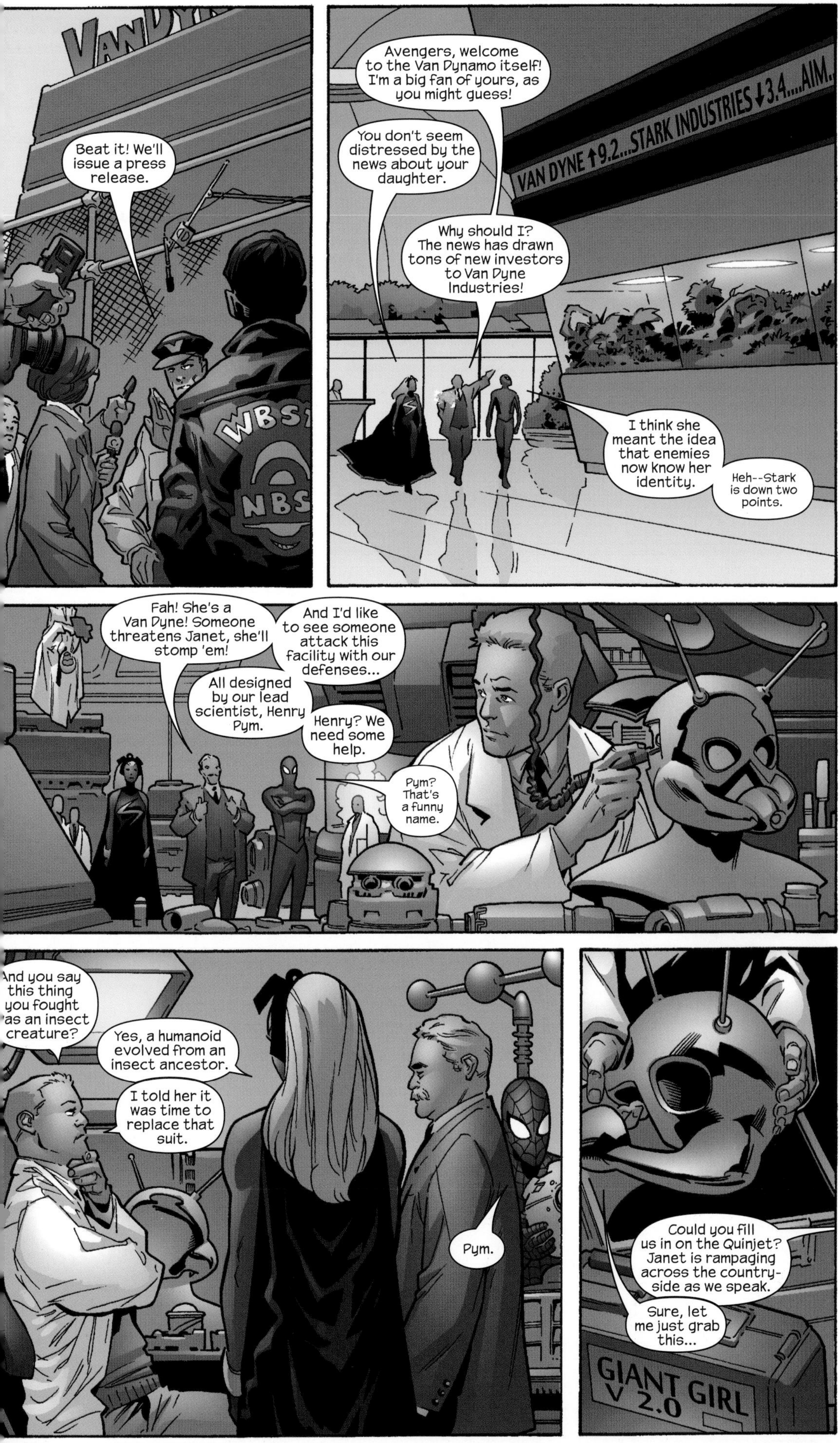
VANDYNE
Beat it! We'll issue a press release.
WBST
NBS
Avengers, welcome to the Van Dynamo itself! I'm a big fan of yours, as you might guess!
VAN DYNE ↑9.2...STARK INDUSTRIES ↓3.4....AIM..
You don't seem distressed by the news about your daughter.
Why should I? The news has drawn tons of new investors to Van Dyne Industries!
I think she meant the idea that enemies now know her identity.
Heh--Stark is down two points.
Fah! She's a Van Dyne! Someone threatens Janet, she'll stomp 'em!
And I'd like to see someone attack this facility with our defenses...
All designed by our lead scientist, Henry Pym.
Henry? We need some help.
Pym? That's a funny name.
And you say this thing you fought was an insect creature?
Yes, a humanoid evolved from an insect ancestor.
I told her it was time to replace that suit.
Pym.
Could you fill us in on the Quinjet? Janet is rampaging across the country-side as we speak.
Sure, let me just grab this...
GIANT GIRL V 2.0

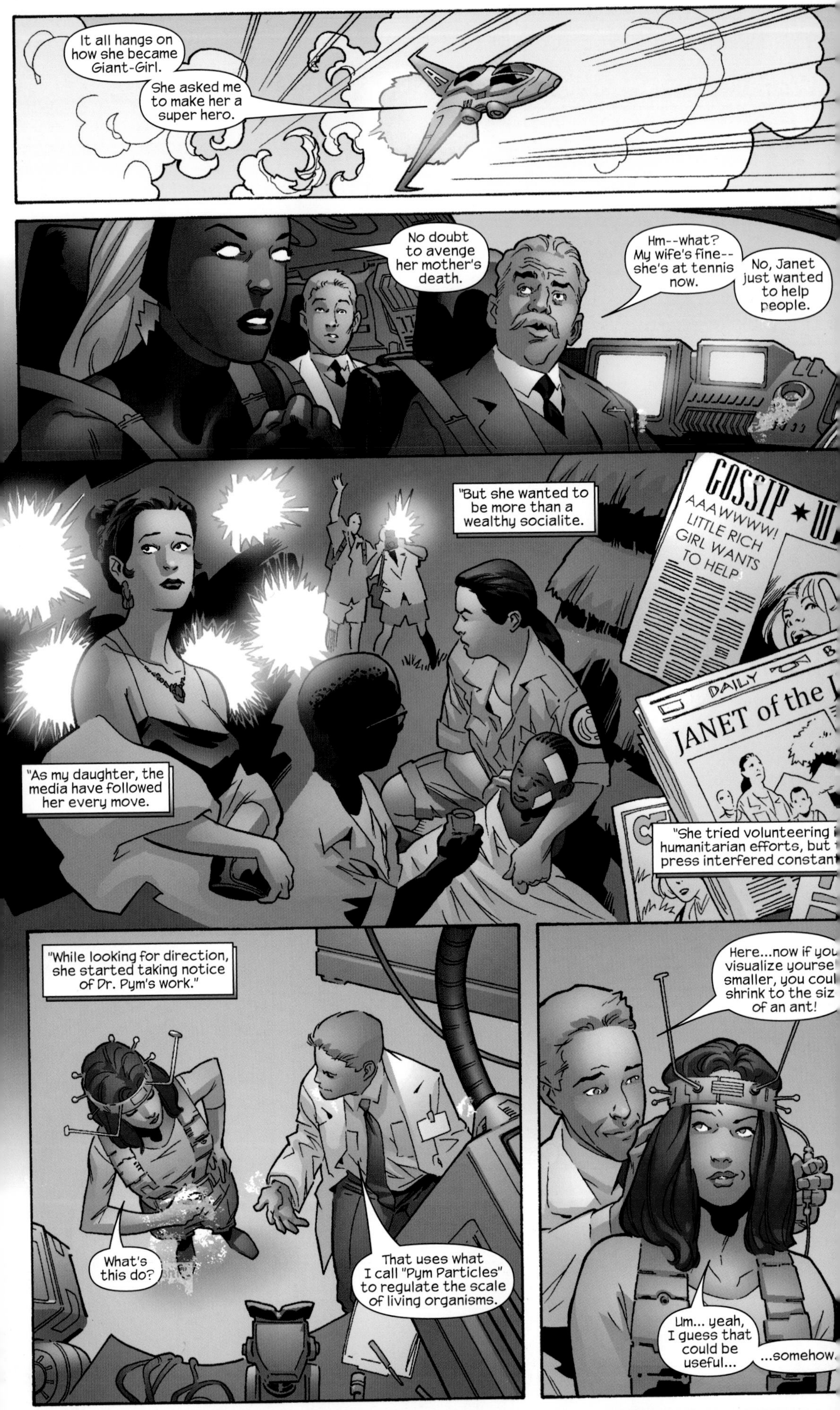
It all hangs on how she became Giant-Girl.
She asked me to make her a super hero.
No doubt to avenge her mother's death.
Hm--what? My wife's fine-- she's at tennis now.
No, Janet just wanted to help people.
"But she wanted to be more than a wealthy socialite.
GOSSIP
AAAWWWW! LITTLE RICH GIRL WANTS TO HELP
DAILY
JANET of the
"As my daughter, the media have followed her every move.
"She tried volunteering humanitarian efforts, but press interfered constant
"While looking for direction, she started taking notice of Dr. Pym's work."
What's this do?
That uses what I call "Pym Particles" to regulate the scale of living organisms.
Here...now if you visualize yourse smaller, you coul shrink to the siz of an ant!
Um... yeah, I guess that could be useful...
...somehow.

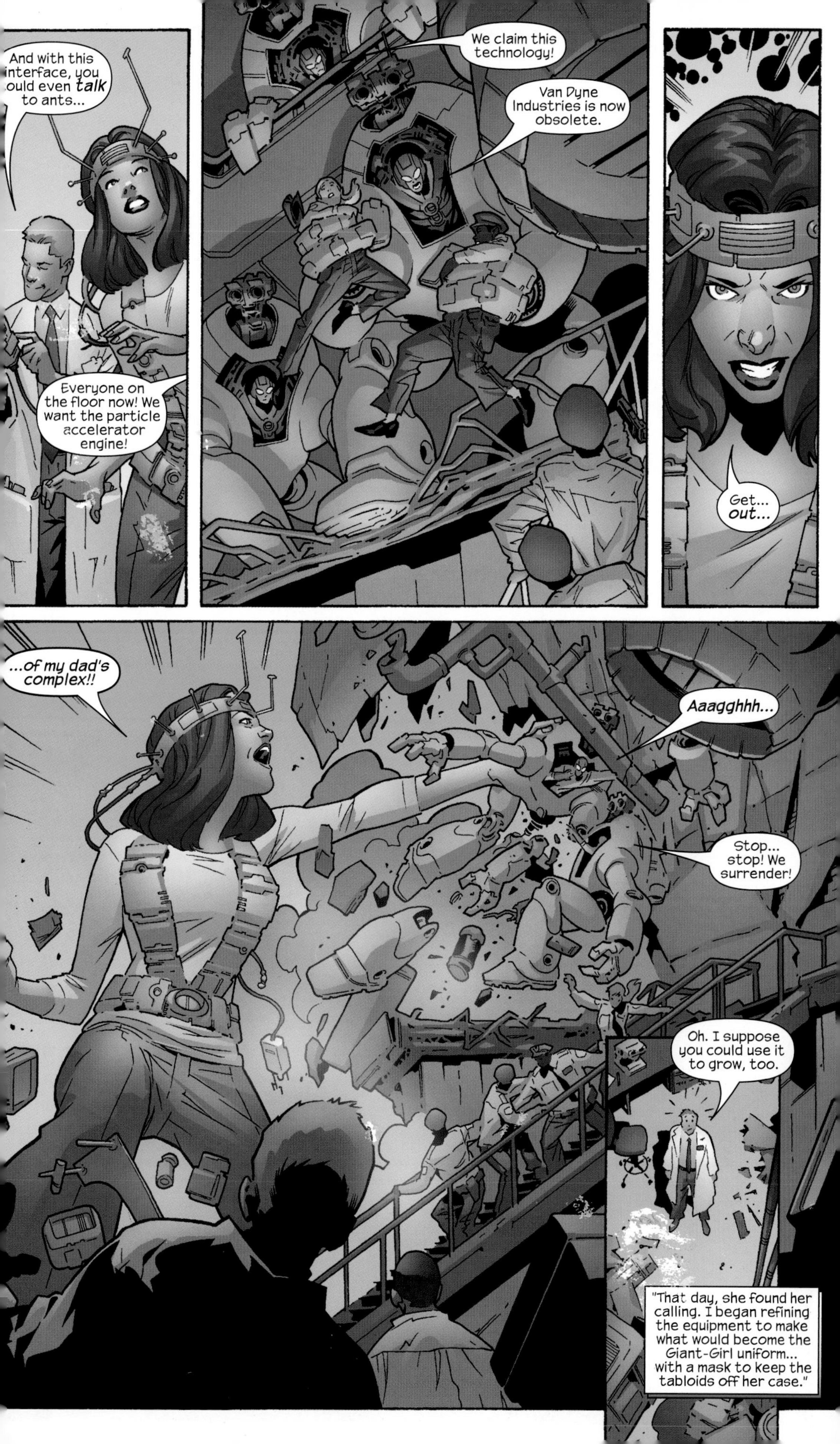
And with this interface, you ould even *talk* to ants...
Everyone on the floor now! We want the particle accelerator engine!
We claim this technology!
Van Dyne Industries is now obsolete.
Get... *out...*
...of my dad's complex!!
Aaagghhh...
Stop... stop! We surrender!
Oh. I suppose you could use it to grow, too.
"That day, she found her calling. I began refining the equipment to make what would become the Giant-Girl uniform... with a mask to keep the tabloids off her case."

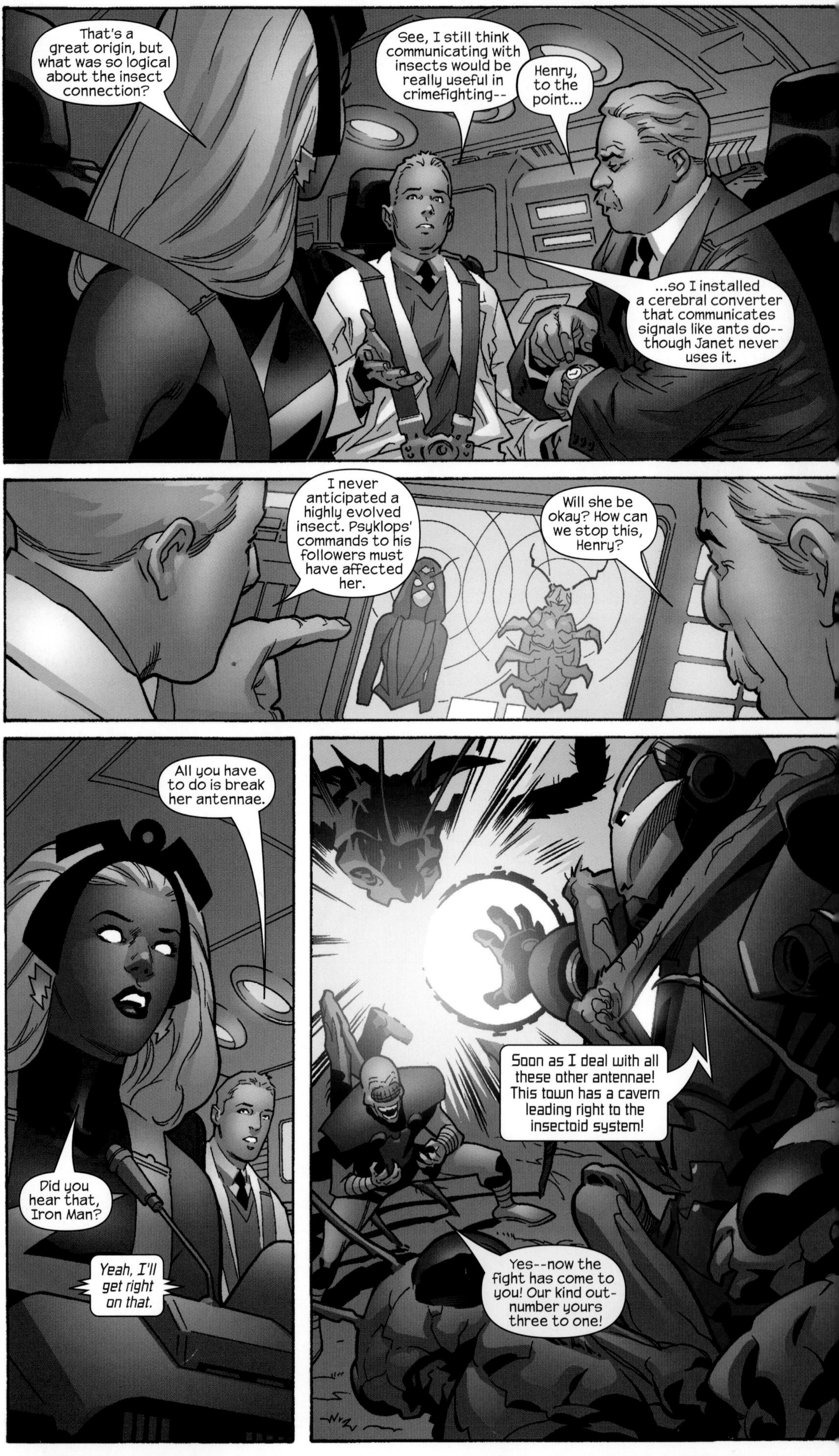
That's a great origin, but what was so logical about the insect connection?
See, I still think communicating with insects would be really useful in crimefighting--
Henry, to the point...
...so I installed a cerebral converter that communicates signals like ants do--though Janet never uses it.
I never anticipated a highly evolved insect. Psyklops' commands to his followers must have affected her.
Will she be okay? How can we stop this, Henry?
All you have to do is break her antennae.
Did you hear that, Iron Man?
Yeah, I'll get right on that.
Soon as I deal with all these other antennae! This town has a cavern leading right to the insectoid system!
Yes--now the fight has come to you! Our kind outnumber yours three to one!

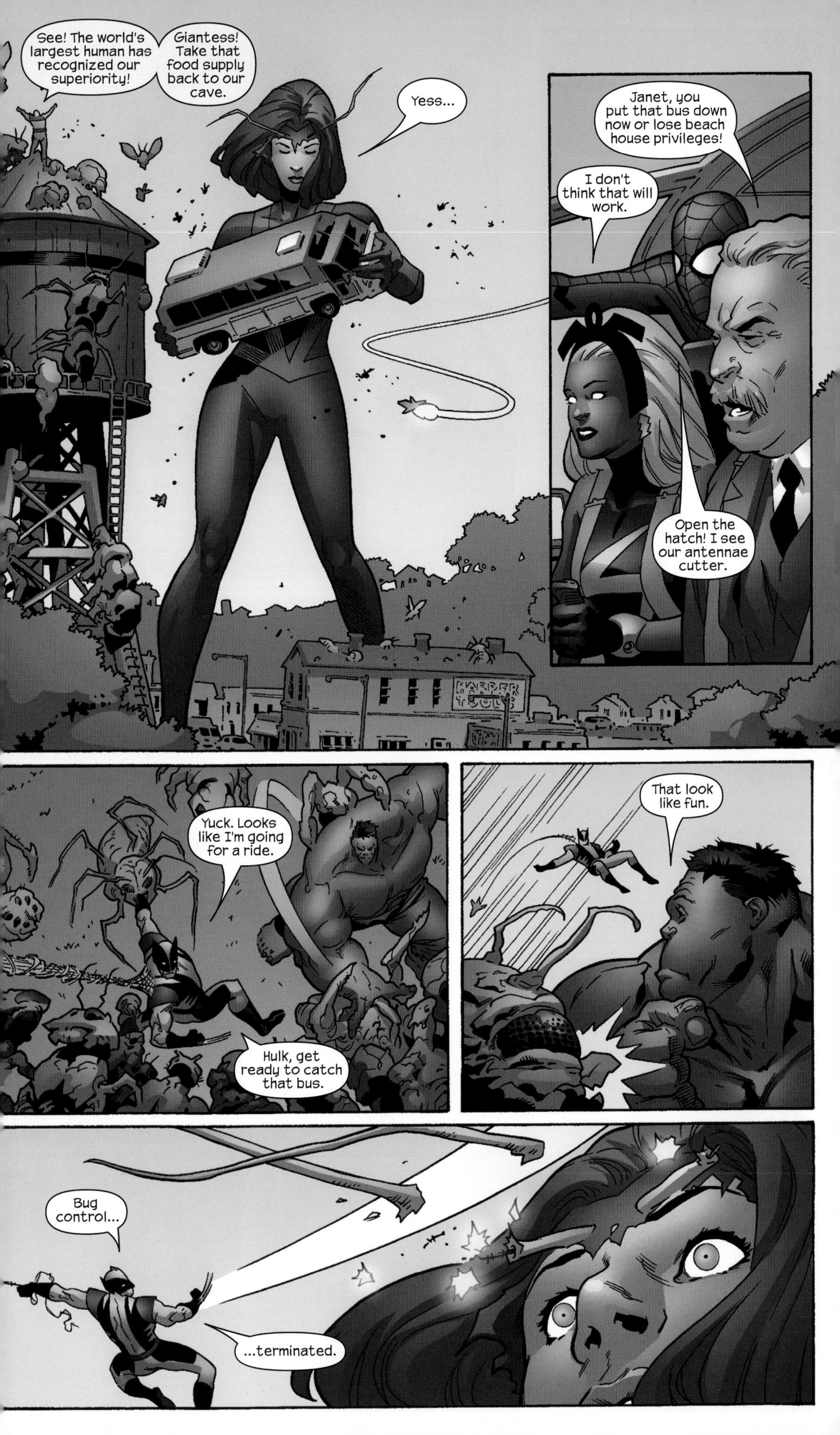
See! The world's largest human has recognized our superiority!
Giantess! Take that food supply back to our cave.
Yess...
Janet, you put that bus down now or lose beach house privileges!
I don't think that will work.
Open the hatch! I see our antennae cutter.
Yuck. Looks like I'm going for a ride.
Hulk, get ready to catch that bus.
That look like fun.
Bug control...
...terminated.

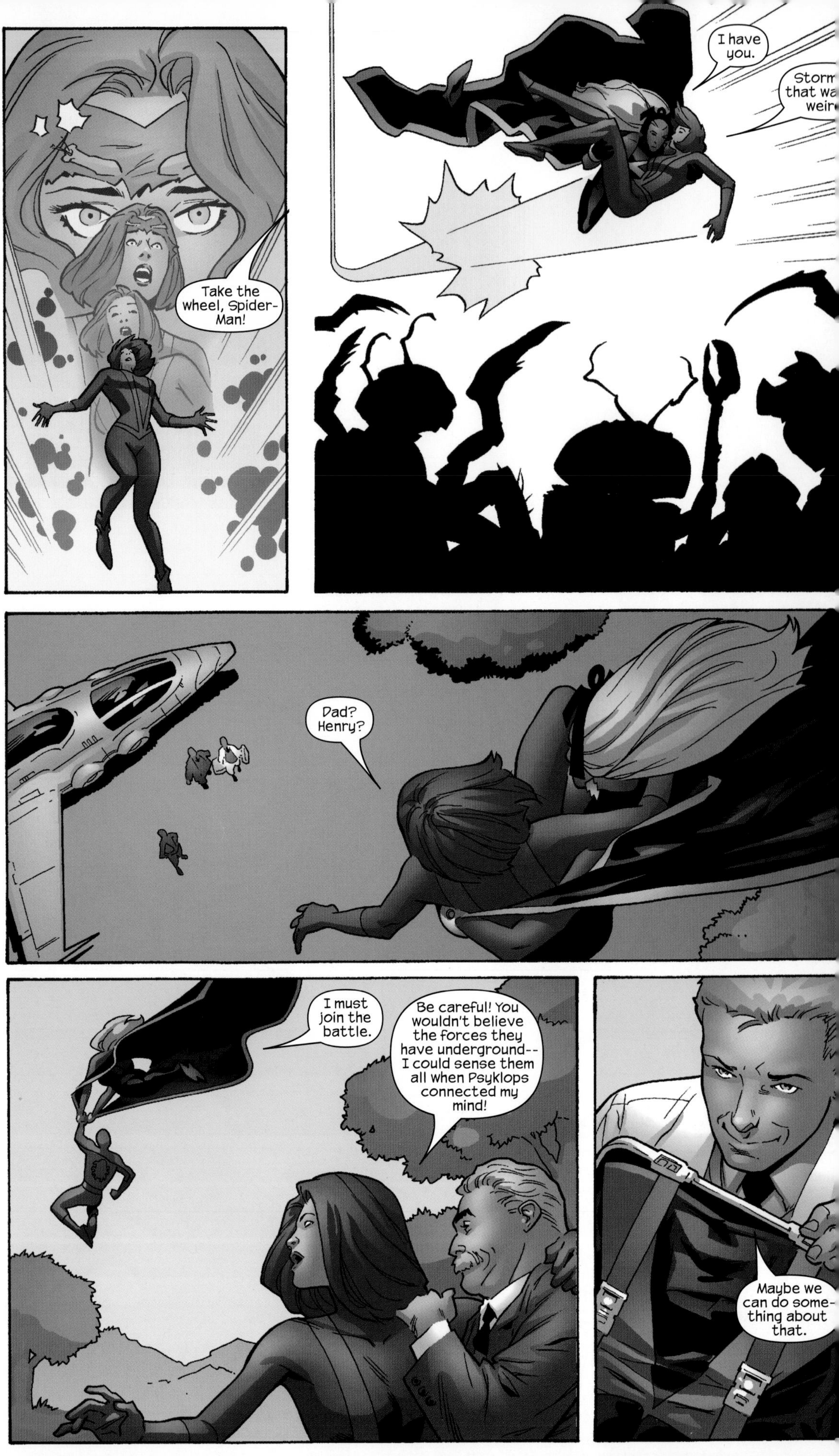
Take the wheel, Spider-Man!
I have you.
Dad? Henry?
I must join the battle.
Be careful! You wouldn't believe the forces they have underground-- I could sense them all when Psyklops connected my mind!
Maybe we can do something about that.

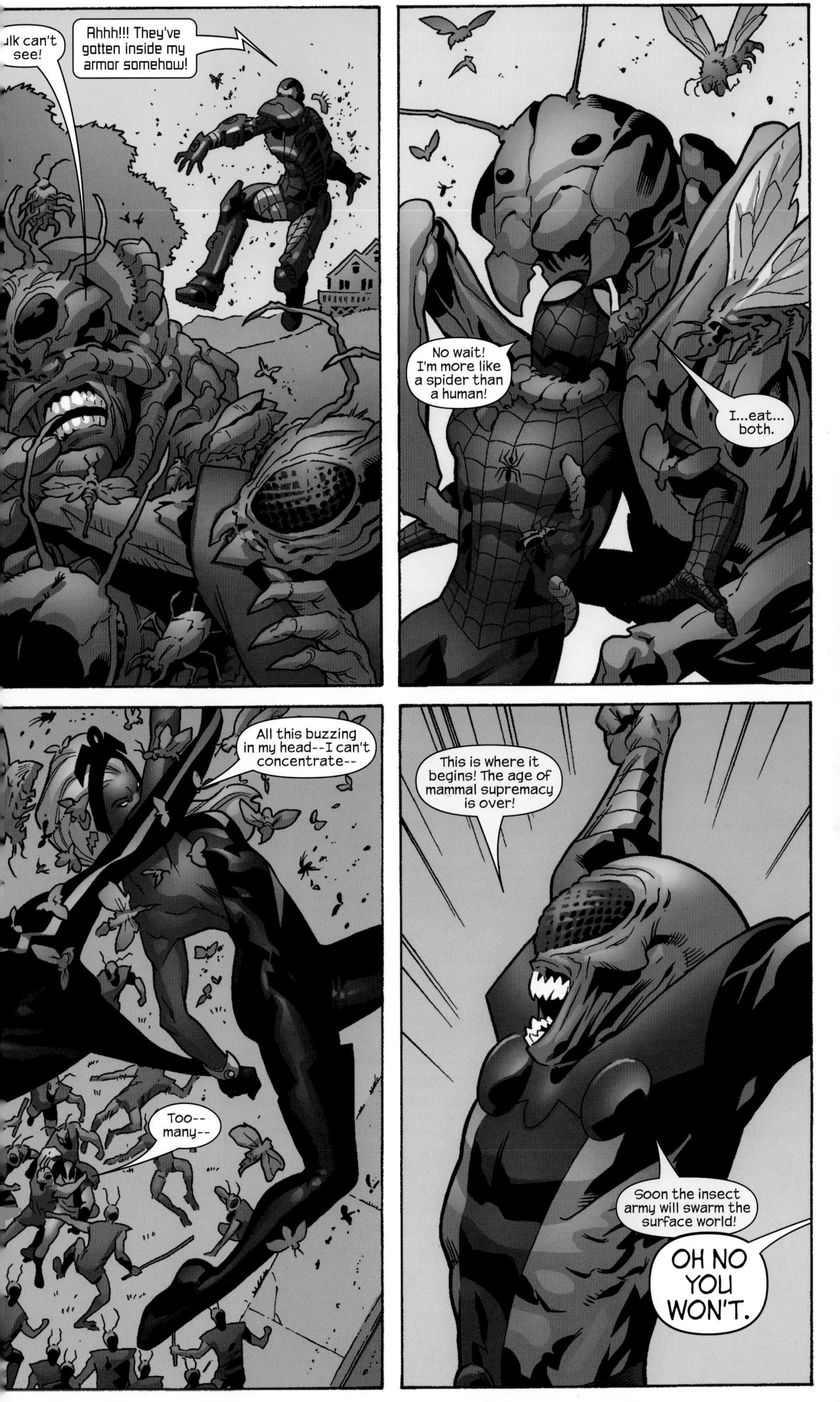
ulk can't see!
Ahhh!!! They've gotten inside my armor somehow!
No wait! I'm more like a spider than a human!
I...eat... both.
All this buzzing in my head--I can't concentrate--
Too-- many--
This is where it begins! The age of mammal supremacy is over!
Soon the insect army will swarm the surface world!
OH NO YOU WON'T.

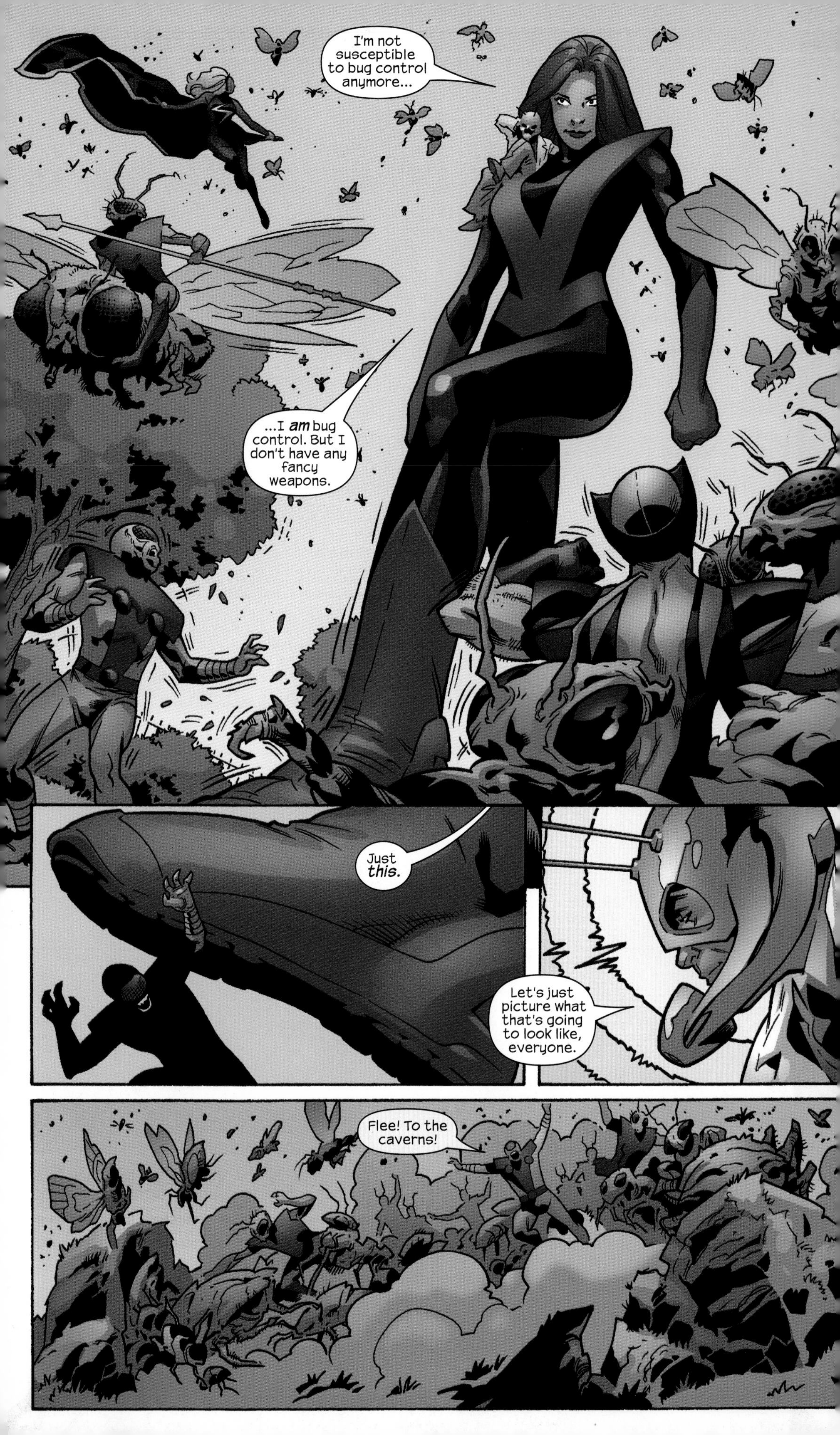
I'm not susceptible to bug control anymore...
...I *am* bug control. But I don't have any fancy weapons.
Just *this.*
Let's just picture what that's going to look like, everyone.
Flee! To the caverns!

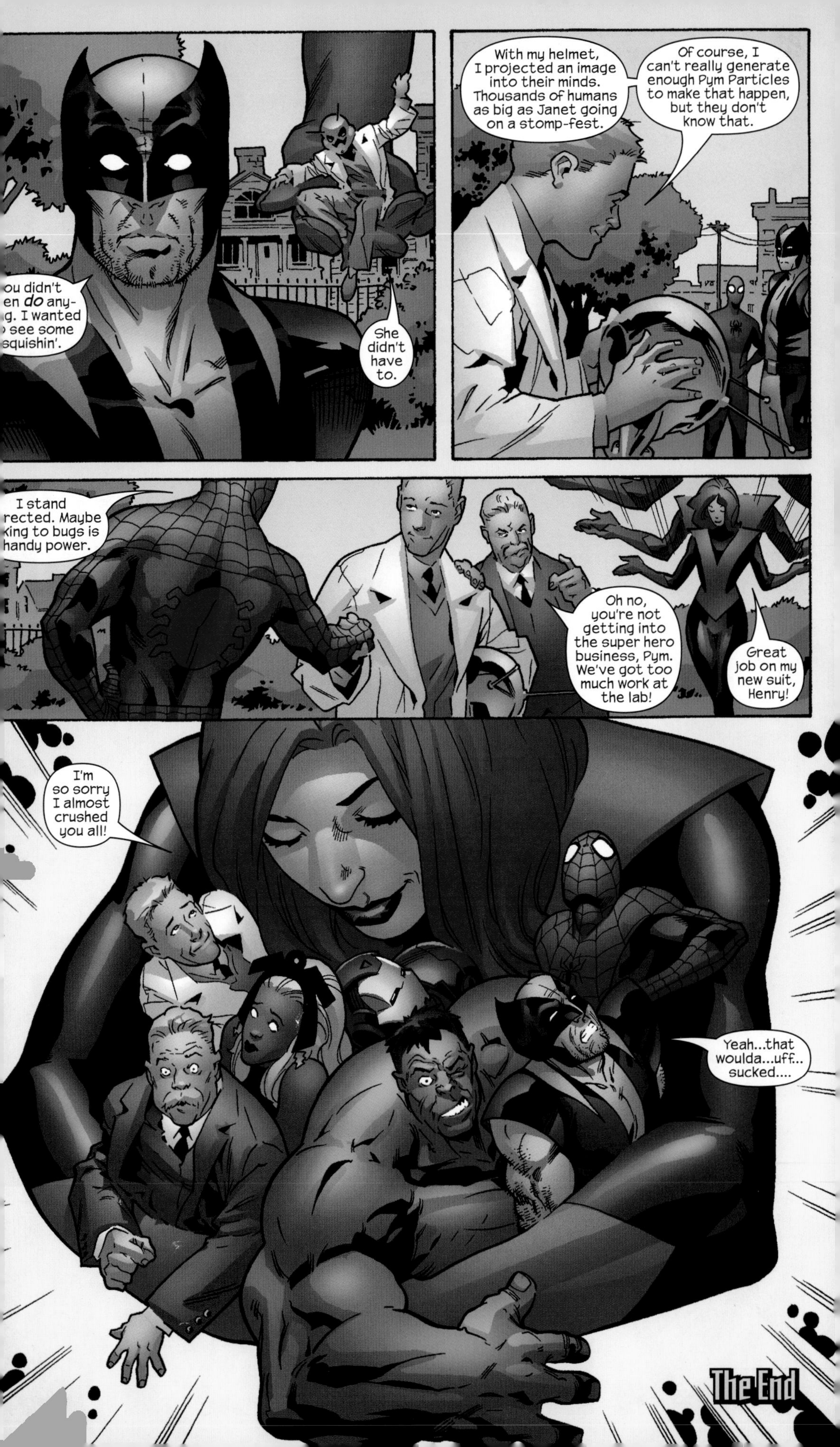
ou didn't en do any- g. I wanted see some squishin'.
She didn't have to.
With my helmet, I projected an image into their minds. Thousands of humans as big as Janet going on a stomp-fest.
Of course, I can't really generate enough Pym Particles to make that happen, but they don't know that.
I stand rected. Maybe king to bugs is handy power.
Oh no, you're not getting into the super hero business, Pym. We've got too much work at the lab!
Great job on my new suit, Henry!
I'm so sorry I almost crushed you all!
Yeah...that woulda...uff... sucked....
The End

THE AVENGERS COLLECT THEM AL

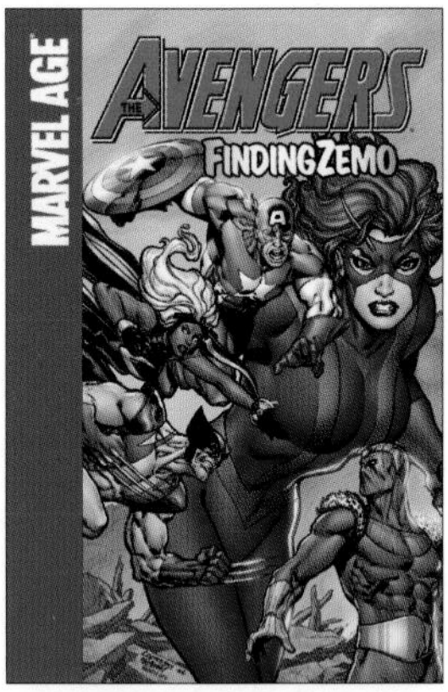
MARVEL AGE
THE AVENGERS
FINDING ZEMO

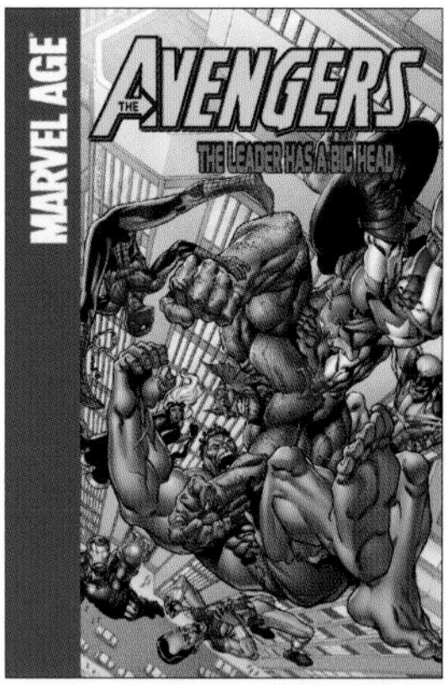
MARVEL AGE
THE AVENGERS
THE LEADER HAS A BIG HEAD

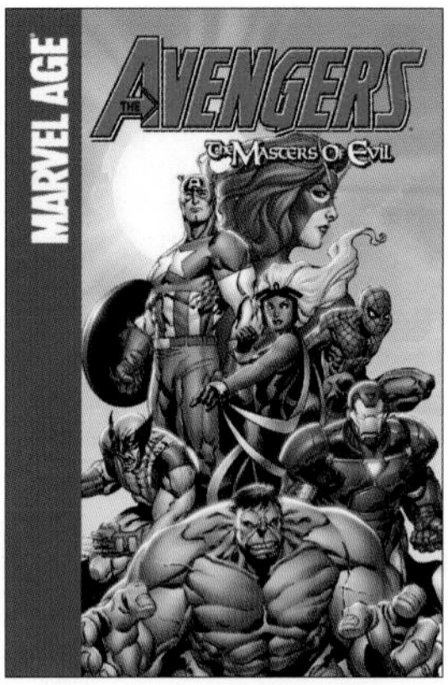
MARVEL AGE
THE AVENGERS
THE MASTERS OF EVIL

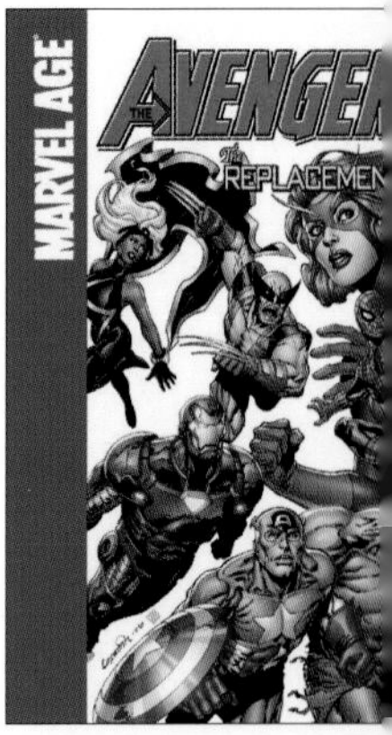
MARVEL AGE
THE

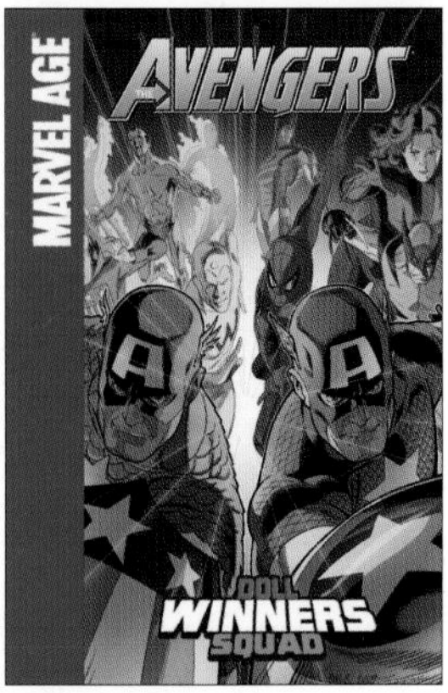
MARVEL AGE
THE AVENGERS
WINNERS
SQUAD

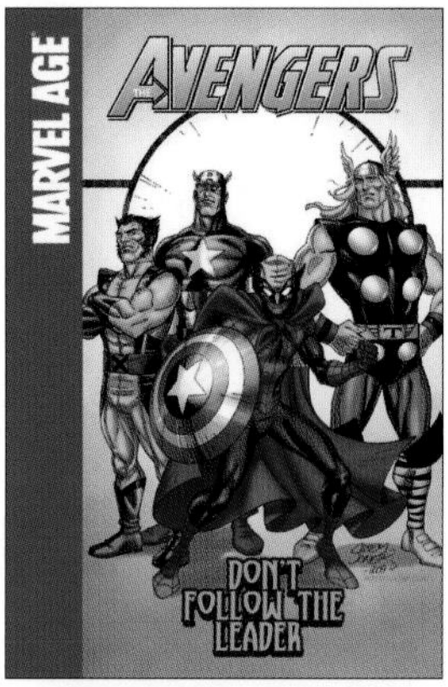
MARVEL AGE
THE AVENGERS
DON'T FOLLOW THE LEADER

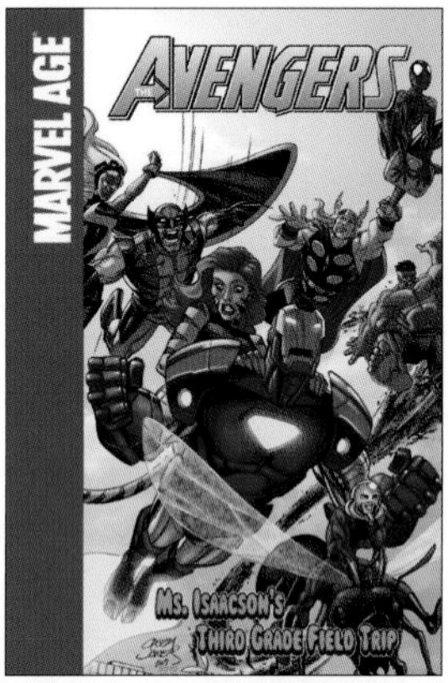
MARVEL AGE
THE AVENGERS
MS. ISAACSON'S THIRD GRADE FIELD TRIP

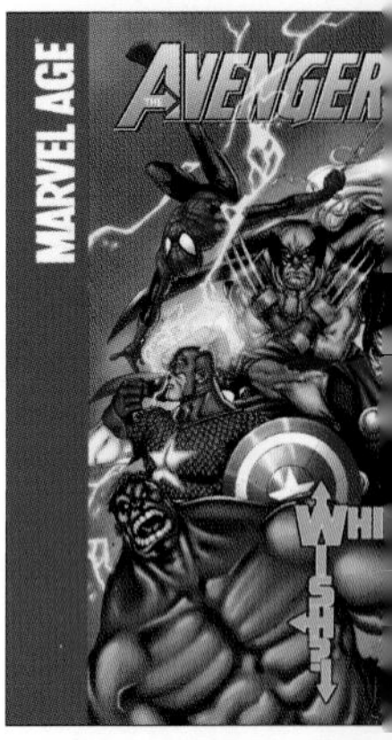
MARVEL AGE
THE

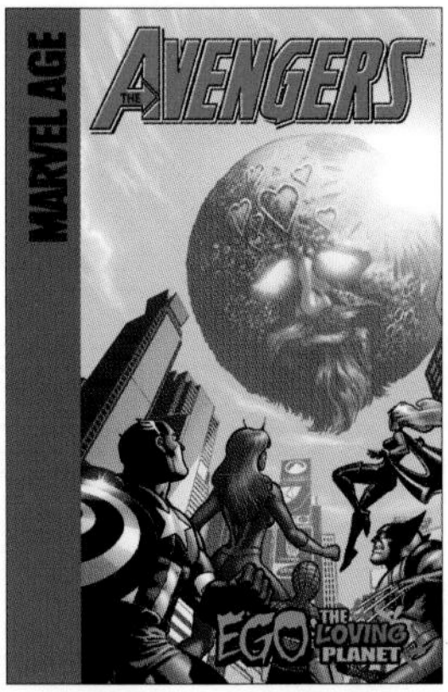
MARVEL AGE
THE AVENGERS
EGO THE LOVING PLANET

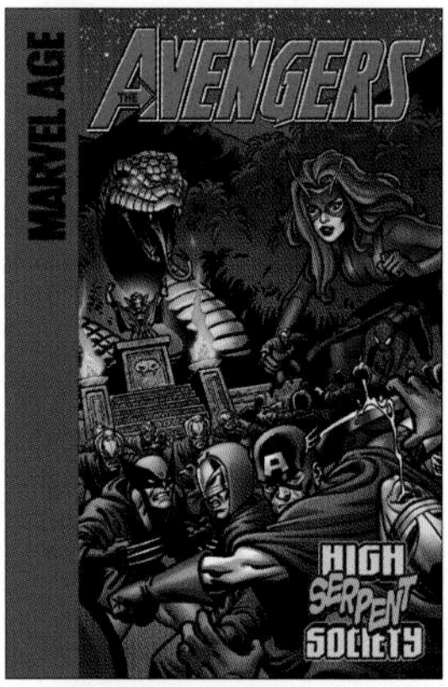
MARVEL AGE
THE AVENGERS
HIGH SERPENT SOCIETY

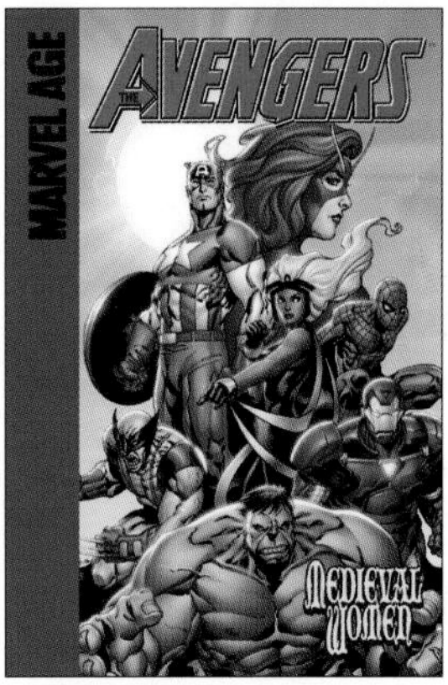
MARVEL AGE
THE AVENGERS
MEDIEVAL WOMEN

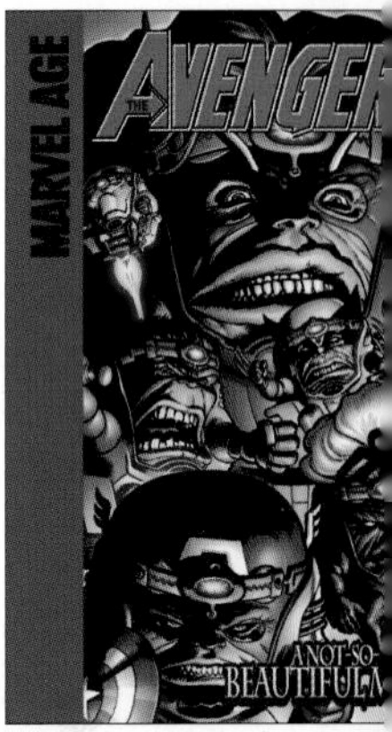
MARVEL AGE
THE
A NOT-SO-

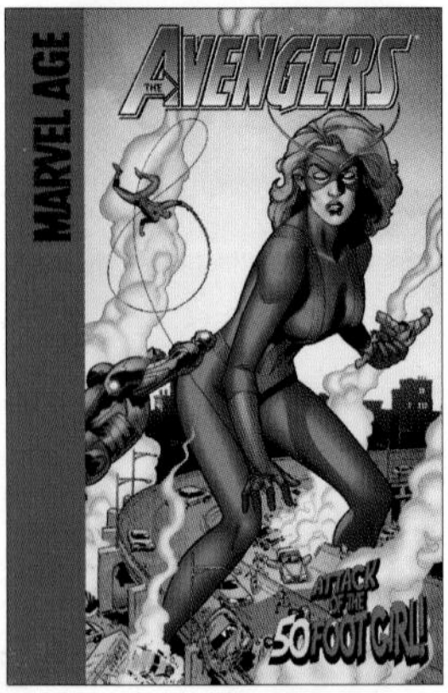
MARVEL AGE
THE AVENGERS
ATTACK OF THE 50-FOOT GIRL!

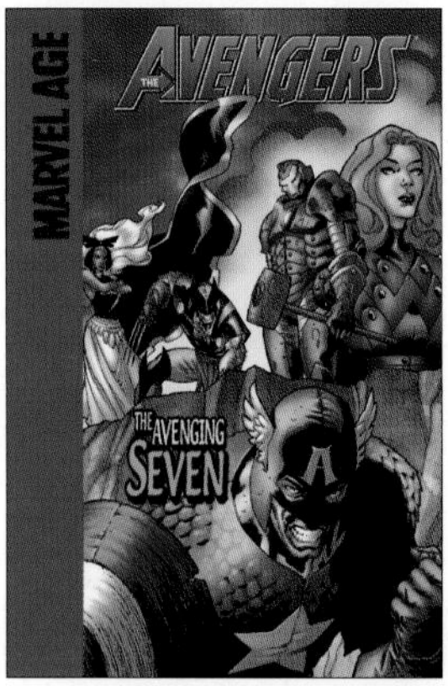
MARVEL AGE
THE AVENGERS
THE AVENGING SEVEN

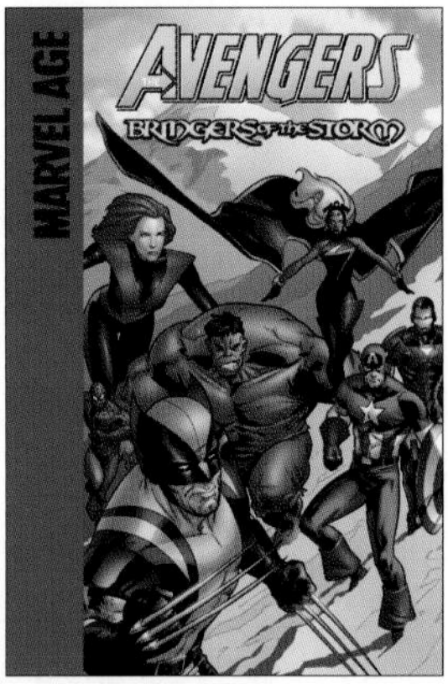
MARVEL AGE
AVENGERS
BRINGERS OF THE STORM

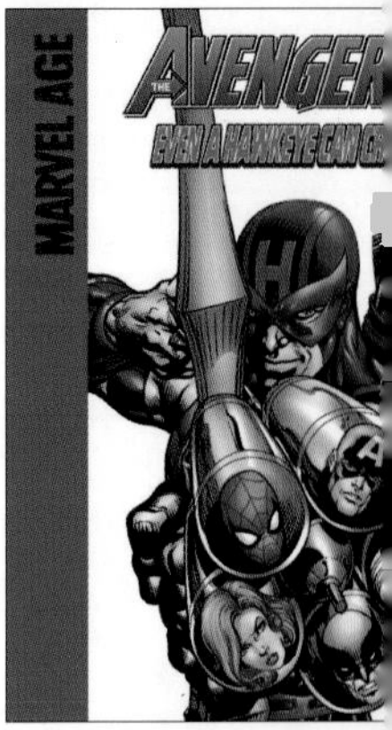
MARVEL AGE